I'M A MIDNIGHT SNACKER!

MEET A VAMPIRE

Lisa Bullard

illustrated by Chiara Buccheri

M MILLBROOK PRESS • MINNEAPOLIS

For Nadine —LB

For my father, who is wiser than the oldest
vampire in history —CB

Millbrook Press
A division of Lerner Publishing Group, Inc.
241 First Avenue North
Minneapolis, MN 55401 USA

For reading levels and more information, look up this title at www.lernerbooks.com.

Main body text set in Sunshine Regular 17/24.
Typeface provided by Chank.

Library of Congress Cataloging-in-Publication Data

Bullard, Lisa.
    I'm a midnight snacker! : Meet a vampire / by Lisa Bullard ;
illustrated by Chiara Buccheri.
       pages   cm. — (Monster Buddies)
    Includes index.
    ISBN 978-0-7613-9191-3 (lib. bdg. : alk. paper)
    ISBN 978-1-4677-4778-3 (eBook)
    1. Vampires—Juvenile literature. I. Title.
BF1556.B85 2015
398'.45—dc23   2013034238

Manufactured in the United States of America
1 – BOL – 7/15/14

TABLE OF CONTENTS

Meet a Vampire

It's the darkest part of night. I sneak out of my castle to go hunting. But I'm not looking for animals. I hunt humans!

My name is Drake, and I'm a vampire.

Vampires are monsters that drink human blood. We once were dead, but we came back to life. After sundown, we search for necks to nibble.

Ruling the Night

Should you wear a fang-proof scarf after dark? No!
Vampires aren't real. We bite people on movie screens. We
drink blood in scary stories. But we're only make-believe.
You will never feel the touch of my cold, dead fingers.

During the day, I sleep in my coffin. Once the sun sets, I go looking for blood. My black hair blends into the darkness. I hide my fangs behind my cape. I glide through the shadows. But I don't cast a shadow of my own. My reflection doesn't show up in mirrors, either.

Vampires are good hunters. I'm stronger and faster than humans. And after a look in my eyes, people follow my orders. I can control rats and wolves too. Plus, if I want to fly, I just turn into a bat.

No long lines at the airport for me!

Fight Back

So how did I become a fright of the night? I was bitten by another vampire.

Good-bye, bunk bed. Hello, coffin!

Some of my friends turned into bloodsuckers in other ways. Vinnie is the seventh son of a seventh son. Valerie ate the meat of a sheep that a wolf had attacked.

I'm really good at being a bad guy. But there are ways you can fight back. You can stop me by putting a stake through my heart. Sunlight burns my skin. And I hate garlic. Yuck, that smell!

I also can't come into your house unless you invite me in. And here's a cool trick if you go out at night. Throw a bunch of seeds on the ground. I love to count things! While I'm shouting out numbers, you'll have time to run.

Dracula's Family

People have shared vampire stories for thousands of years. Long ago, people didn't understand sickness and death. So they told tales about monsters. They tried to explain scary events with these stories.

Later storytellers might have known about animals that drink blood. Vampire bats fly around Central America and South America. They feed on the blood of other animals—or even humans! But the bats usually bite people's big toes, not their necks.

Speaking of stories, have you met my relatives? The most famous one is Count Dracula. He's from a book Bram Stoker wrote in 1897. Or maybe you know Count von Count? He's the number lover on *Sesame Street*.

john smith

1904–1960

My cousins in Greece have the heads and upper bodies of a woman. But they have the lower bodies of snakes. My Australian cousins suck blood through their fingers and toes.

Look into My Eyes

Remember, there's no need to worry about vampires. These monsters aren't real. It's safe to go out after dark.

Now look into my eyes and obey my words.
First, bend your neck this way . . .

A Vampire's Day Writing Activity

You've learned a lot about vampires. Now it's time to show off some fang facts. Grab a pencil and a piece of paper. Write a short story about a night in the life of a vampire. Does he visit his vampire cousins around the world? Does he hang out in a bat cave? Draw a picture to go with your story.

GLOSSARY

coffin: a long, narrow box in which people are buried after they die

fang: a long, sharp tooth

garlic: a strong-smelling plant used to flavor food

reflection: the image that you can see in a mirror

stake: a pointed wooden pole

TO LEARN MORE

Books

Howe, James. *Rabbit-cadabra!* New York: Simon Spotlight, 2007.
It's time for the school magic show. Will a magician pull Bunnicula the vampire rabbit out of a hat?

Pace, Anne Marie. *Vampirina Ballerina.* New York: Disney Hyperion Books, 2012.
Do vampires get stage fright? Find out in this fun picture book about a vampire who was born to dance.

Somervill, Barbara A. *Vampire Bats: Hunting for Blood.* New York: PowerKids Press, 2008.
Learn how vampire bats feast on the blood of other animals.

Websites

National Geographic: Bats—Vampire Bats
http://video.nationalgeographic.com/video/animals/mammals-animals/bats/bat_vampire_feeding
Visit this website for some facts about and footage of vampire bats.

Sesame Street: Count von Count
http://www.sesamestreet.org/muppets/count-von-count
At this site, you'll find videos and coloring sheets about the famous counting vampire.

INDEX